D0113815

The Fifteenth
Peanut Butter Sandwich

The Fifteenth Peanut Butter Sandwich

by Marjorie Kaplan

illustrated by Eileen McKeating

Four Winds Press
New York

Text copyright © 1990 by Marjorie Kaplan
Illustrations copyright © 1990 by Eileen McKeating
All rights reserved. No part of this book may be reproduced or
transmitted in any form or by any means, electronic or mechanical,
including photocopying, recording, or by any information storage and
retrieval system, without permission in writing from the Publisher.
Four Winds Press
Macmillan Publishing Company
866 Third Avenue, New York, NY 10022
Collier Macmillan Canada, Inc.
First Edition
Printed in the United States of America

10 9 8 7 6 5 4 3 2 1

The text of this book is set in 12 point Plantin Light.
The illustrations are rendered in pencil.

Library of Congress Cataloging-in-Publication Data
Kaplan, Marjorie.
The fifteenth peanut butter sandwich / Marjorie Kaplan;
illustrated by Eileen McKeating. — 1st ed.   p.   cm.
Summary: Only a constant supply of peanut butter sandwiches
helps when eight-year-old Kathy tries to find a temporary home for
her cat Romeo while her family moves to England for a year.
ISBN 0-02-749350-4
[1. Cats—Fiction. 2. Moving, Household—Fiction.]
I. McKeating, Eileen, ill. II. Title. III. Title:
15th peanut butter sandwich.
PZ7.K1294Fi 1990 [E]—dc20   89-32784 CIP AC

For Lucy and Nathan

1

On May second, during Kathy's lunch hour, her dad brought home such a giant problem for Romeo that for a while Kathy was afraid there weren't enough peanut butter sandwiches in the world to solve it.

Kathy was sitting at the table, eating a chocolate chip cookie and arranging violets in a jug at the same time. Romeo, who had spring fever, had climbed up on her lap and gone to sleep, his paws curled under his chin. He didn't seem to notice the cookie crumbs that fell on Kathy's blue jeans and into his yellow striped fur. Kathy's mom had come home to lunch, too. She was sitting at the table studying a computer printout sheet while she ate her pasta salad.

Kathy's dad drove up into the driveway, parked the car, and rushed into the house, leaving the front door open. The smell of honeysuckle and newly cut grass filled the room. Kathy ran to meet him with Romeo under her arm. Her father picked her up and twirled her around. He had played basketball when he was young, so he never dropped her.

"I can't stay," he said. "I just wanted to tell you the good news. The company is sending us to London for the year. We leave June first."

Mrs. Spry jumped up from the table and hugged her husband, who was still holding Kathy, who was holding on to Romeo, who was hanging on for dear life. Romeo never liked being twirled around.

"I've always wanted to see Queen Elizabeth and the lord mayor of London," Kathy's mother said. "I wonder if either of them needs a computer programmer."

"We'll see," Mr. Spry said. "But now I have to go back to work."

He put Kathy down. Romeo jumped out of Kathy's arms and went to sit on the windowsill under the bottom ruffle of the curtain.

"I wonder how Romeo will like London," Kathy said when she had caught her breath.

Her father turned to go.

"That's no problem," he said over his shoulder. "England has very strict rules about animals. Romeo can't go to London. We'll rent him out with the house."

Kathy went over and pulled Romeo out from under the curtain. She patted his back.

"In that case," she said, "I vote against this family's going to London. Romeo is not a cat that one rents out with a house."

Her father stopped with his hand on the doorknob. His gray eyes looked straight into Kathy's green speckled ones.

"Honeybunch, we're not staying home from London for any cat," he said.

And that was that.

"Romeo will be happier here with his friends," her dad said, sounding a little nicer.

Kathy wanted to stamp her foot. Instead she stamped her big toe inside her tennis shoe.

"But Romeo doesn't have any friends besides us," she wailed.

"She's right," Mrs. Spry said. "The people on this block don't know one tabby cat from another."

Kathy's dad didn't argue. He couldn't tell one cat from another himself, tabby or not.

"I meant his cat friends," he said.

Kathy sat down next to her mother. They both laughed so hard at the idea of Romeo's cat friends that they knocked the printout sheet into the pasta salad. Romeo got along worse with cats than with people. Whenever another cat came into the yard, Romeo spit, hissed, and fought tooth and claw. He didn't have one cat friend in the world, and what was more, he didn't want one.

Kathy's father was too happy to notice they weren't

laughing a nice laugh. He almost danced out the door, as if he were dribbling a basketball.

"Jolly good. Cheerio. I'll pop back in time for tea."

Kathy sat very still after he left. She wasn't hungry anymore.

"It's only a year," her mother said.

"A year is a very, very long time," Kathy said as she thought about the Fourth of July, Halloween, Christmas, Valentine's Day, and Easter.

"Some years last a very short time," Mrs. Spry replied.

2

The next day at lunchtime, Kathy opened a big jar of peanut butter. She breathed deeply. Kathy planned to invent a peanut butter perfume someday. She dug into the smooth swirl across the top and made Peanut Butter Sandwich #1 for Romeo's new problem. She put the sandwich into a plastic bag, placed it in the bottom of a basket, set Romeo in on top of the sandwich, and carried the basket out to the curb to think about Romeo's problem.

Kathy always ate peanut butter sandwiches when Romeo had a problem. They helped her to think. The biggest problem Romeo had ever had was an Eight Peanut Butter Sandwich problem, and Kathy had never forgotten it.

Long ago, when she had started in first grade, she had had to decide what Romeo would do all day while she was gone. She had eaten seven peanut butter sandwiches, and had swallowed the second-to-last bite of PBS8 (as she called it), before she had decided that Romeo should curl up and go to sleep when she left

for school, and then the two of them would play extra hard when she came home.

Romeo had liked that idea. But she knew he wouldn't like to sleep for a whole year, even if he could.

Romeo climbed out over the side of Kathy's basket and rubbed his face on her leg. Kathy could see that he was worried.

"Don't worry, Romeo," she said as she reached in for her sandwich. "There is an answer to every problem a cat has, if one can only think of it."

Romeo jumped up on her lap and went to sleep.

Just as she swallowed the last bit of PBS1, Kathy had an idea! She stood up so fast that Romeo barely had time to leap to the ground. He turned around and frowned at her.

"Sorry, Romeo," Kathy said. "But I just had an idea."

That evening she asked for a piece of her mother's best writing paper. She drew lines so light that only she could see them. With a dictionary by her side to look up the hard words, she wrote a letter to the queen of England.

Dear Queen Elizabeth:

Please let my cat, Romeo, come to London with me. I am sure your rules were not meant for

Romeo. He is a noble cat and he may have royal blood in his veins. He is a tabby cat with yellow striped fur. You will not be sorry if you let him come.

Yours truly,
Kathy Spry

P.S. Can I buy peanut butter in London?

She sealed the letter in an envelope and asked her father to mail it from his office.

"How sweet," her mom said.

"Wouldn't it be funny," Kathy said, "if I solved this hard problem with only one peanut butter sandwich?"

Every day at noon, Kathy ran home to see if there was a letter from the queen. Finally on May nineteenth, when Kathy ran into the house to pick up Romeo, her mother handed her a letter from Buckingham Palace.

It was a happy-looking letter with lions and crowns in the corner and an English stamp on the envelope. The paper inside was even nicer than her mom's, and Kathy could tell that the queen had used the royal typewriter. Probably the queen typed better than anyone else in the world! The margins were straight, and there was not one little smudge on the paper.

But the words were very sad. The letter said that

even the queen had to obey the rules about bringing a cat into England.

"However, we do have peanut butter in our shops," she added.

Kathy hugged Romeo.

"I tried, Romeo," she said. "But Queen Elizabeth will not let you come to London."

Kathy went out to the curb to think and to eat PBS2. More than two weeks had passed. She was sorry she'd wasted all that time waiting for Queen Elizabeth to answer her letter. From now on she would sit on the curb and eat a peanut butter sandwich every day until Romeo's problem was solved for sure.

When Kathy was in the middle of PBS2, her dad called and told her mother that he had rented the house for the year. In the middle of her last bite, Kathy had a glimmer of an idea. It was really more like a hope than an idea.

"Maybe they have a girl," she said to Romeo, "who has always wanted a tabby cat of her own since the very first day she was born. I could teach her how to hold you on her lap and how to solve your problems."

Kathy was almost jealous.

That evening as soon as her dad came home, Kathy ran out to meet him. She stood on her toes and put her head in the driver's window before he had a chance to turn off the engine.

"Tell me about the family who is going to rent our house," Kathy said. "Do they have a girl?"

Mr. Spry turned the key, opened the car door, and folded himself up a little bit to get out of the car.

"Do they have a girl?" he repeated, unfolding himself again as he stepped onto the driveway. His head almost touched the overhang of the porch roof.

"Do they have a girl?" he said again. "They have *three* girls, and they all love cats."

Kathy took his hand. "Did they tell you they loved cats?" she asked. Sometimes her father was wrong about cats and people.

"They didn't have to," he said. "They have three little girls and three cats. Each little girl has a cat of her own."

"You must be joking," Kathy said.

She tried to look under his mustache to see if his mouth was trying to hide a smile.

"I never joke about cats," he said. "This was just jolly good luck. Romeo will have the time of his life."

"But Romeo hates cats," Kathy groaned. "He'll spend the whole year spitting, hissing, and fighting tooth and claw. Nothing could be worse."

Mr. Spry stooped down to pick up the evening paper.

12

"Romeo just thinks he hates cats. He'll love the company."

Kathy held Romeo around his stomach and put him under her father's nose.

"Can't you see? Romeo would be the only cat in the house without a girl of his own to hold him on her lap and to solve his problems. A fourth cat in that family would be like a fifth wheel."

Kathy's mom opened the door.

"Tell him he can't do it," Kathy said to her mother. "Tell him he can't rent the house to three girls and three cats."

Mr. Spry kissed Mrs. Spry and sat down to read the newspaper. "I'm sorry, Kathy, but I've already signed the lease," he said.

It all depends on me, Kathy thought. Even her father was no help in this problem.

3

Each day from May twentieth through May twenty-second, Kathy and Romeo spent a long time sitting on the curb. Kathy ate PBS3, PBS4, and PBS5.

On May twenty-third, as she started PBS6, Romeo looked very sad.

"Don't worry, Romeo," Kathy said. "I promised to solve your problem, and I will, no matter what."

Kathy kissed him on the top of his head to show she meant it. She had only one crusty corner of PBS6 left when she got an idea. She didn't jump up for joy this time, however. She didn't like this PBS6 idea one little bit. But a promise was a promise, especially to Romeo, and especially after she had kissed him on the top of his head.

She disliked the PBS6 plan so much that she put off telling her parents about it for three days. Each day she sat down on the curb with Romeo and tried to think of a different plan while she ate the next peanut butter sandwich. But on May twenty-sixth—after PBS9

and just six days before they were going to fly to London—she had to give up. She still had only one plan in her head, the PBS6 plan.

Finally, when Kathy heard the clock strike eight that evening (her family was so busy packing they hadn't started to eat dinner until seven-thirty), she took a deep breath and said, "I have solved our problem."

"Which problem, love?" her father asked as he finished his apple pie, brushed the crumbs off his mustache, and pushed away from the table.

Kathy's mom started to pick up the dishes, and her dad put the food away.

"*The* problem," Kathy said. "The problem of what to do about Romeo."

"That was settled a long time ago, little Kitty-Kathy," her dad said. "Romeo will live right here. He'll hardly know we're gone."

Kathy paid no attention to her father. She kept sitting at the table and staring out the window at the new leaves against the dark sky.

"I have a plan," she said. "This is what I'm going to do."

Suddenly, before Kathy could tell them her plan, she heard a loud *thump, thump, thump.* She looked up at her parents. They had stopped clearing the table and were waiting for her plan, but they didn't seem to hear any thumps. At the same time, Kathy felt a bumping against her chest. She looked down, expecting to see her T-shirt going in and out, but the T-shirt rested quietly all the way down to where it was tucked into her jeans. The thumps and bumps were inside her chest. Only Kathy could hear and feel them.

"I think," Kathy said in a strange little voice that didn't sound like her at all, "I think that I will have to be rented out with the house along with Romeo. Then he'll have a girl of his own to look out for him, to hold him, and to solve his problems. You two will have to go to England without me."

Both of Kathy's parents turned red in the face. Her mother set down the salad bowl and put her arms around Kathy's neck. Her father reached over and picked up Kathy's hand.

"No dice, kid," he said. "We're a package deal. We go together, whether it's to London or to the moon."

He had dropped his pretend English accent for once.

The thumps and bumps stopped. In spite of herself, Kathy felt much better. Her father pulled Kathy's chair away from the table.

"Leave the dishes for the downstairs maid," he said to Mrs. Spry.

That was a joke.

"I need to gather my family around me tonight.

Kathy, I know you are very busy solving problems, but I'm feeling very sad. I wish you'd climb on my lap and comfort me for a few minutes."

So they left the rest of the dishes on the table and went out to the screened porch. Kathy's mother and father sank into the cushions of the rocking chairs. Romeo jumped onto her mother's lap, and Kathy, big as she was, curled up on her father's lap to comfort him.

Mr. Spry pointed to the sky. "That's the same moon that will shine down on us in London."

Kathy began to feel sleepy. She thought of Romeo's problem. Now that she knew how bad it felt to be rented out with a house, she was more determined than ever to solve Romeo's problem for him. But she had so little time. They were leaving in just six days.

"To think," her mom said, "you thought we'd leave you for a whole year with strangers."

"I thought you said a year wasn't so long," Kathy mumbled, almost falling off to sleep.

"Some years aren't," Mrs. Spry said. "It depends on whom you're with, and what you're doing."

So that's it, Kathy thought as she drifted off. I must find a home for Romeo where a year goes fast. I have only six days left.

4

"On our first day in London, we'll go see the Changing of the Guard at Buckingham Palace," Kathy's mother promised at lunchtime the next day.

But Kathy didn't even care. It was already May twenty-seventh and she still hadn't solved Romeo's problem.

"I'm going to spend my lunch hour thinking about a home for Romeo where the time goes fast," Kathy said.

"I'm proud of you," her mother said. "But pick one right on this block where you know everyone, and don't be late for school."

"With people like Mom and the queen of England around, it's a wonder I get any problems solved," Kathy grumbled to herself as she sat down on the curb to eat her sandwich.

Romeo climbed onto her lap. Each hair of his coat picked up the light of the sun. Kathy rubbed her hand over his back.

"One thing you can't do, Romeo, is stay in a house

that already has a cat. He is bound to be jealous of you. We have to find you a family without any cats of their own."

The next day was a Saturday. Kathy sat on the curb and decided she would have to find a house with at least one child to take care of Romeo.

"Children understand a cat's problems much better than grown-ups do," she told her mother. "Grown-ups must forget."

"You do not know all children," her mother said, "nor all adults."

"Nor do I have time to know them," Kathy said to Romeo.

That evening Kathy started to make a list. She headed it: CHILDREN—YES   CATS—NO. But then she could find only one family on the block to put on the list, a family who lived right next door, the Youngs. They had six children and no cats.

But Kathy thought about the Young family the whole next day. She was worried about Rosemary Young, the family's large Labrador retriever. When Rosemary had first moved into the Youngs' house, she had sat at the picture window and barked each time Romeo passed. Romeo didn't like her, and what was worse, Rosemary didn't like Romeo. What would happen when they met? That had been Romeo's problem then.

It had taken two peanut butter sandwiches for Kathy to solve it.

"Romeo," she had said finally, "Rosemary Young is too big a dog for you to tangle with. Her feelings may change in time. But for now, when you see Rosemary outside on the sidewalk, you climb the nearest tree."

And that is exactly what Romeo had done ever since.

But on May thirtieth, Memorial Day, Kathy decided that it would be easier for Romeo to get along with Rosemary than with the three strange cats and the three strange girls who were going to live at Kathy's house. The Young family was composed of Mr. and Mrs. Young, Baby Jasper, and five noisy big boys who had gone fishing with their dad early that morning. There was bound to be someone to hold Romeo and to solve his problems. Perhaps Mrs. Young would like to hold Romeo herself when Baby Jasper was crawling around on the floor.

"Rosemary may be a bit hard to get along with at first," Kathy said to Romeo. He was lying in the basket with his head resting on the edge as they walked to the Youngs' house at lunchtime. "But she'll come around when she gets to know you. You will be close to your own home and you'll have six boys to play with. Best of all, the Youngs have no cats. The days will fly by."

Mr. Young had built a six-foot-high stockade fence around the house after they got Rosemary. Sometimes Kathy climbed over the fence, just as the boys did, but today she opened the gate because she was carrying her basket. Since the five big boys had gone fishing, the house seemed very quiet. Kathy walked up to the porch and looked through the draperies, which Rosemary had chewed to shreds. Pretty, red-haired Mrs. Young was sitting on the couch reading a magazine. She looked lonesome to Kathy, all by herself in the empty living room. Kathy rang the bell.

Mrs. Young opened the door just a few inches. Rosemary bounded into the living room and began to bark, *"Woof, woof."*

"Why, Kathy," Mrs. Young said above Rosemary's woofs.

"Mommee-ee," Kathy heard Baby Jasper wail.

"Bad dog," Mrs. Young said to Rosemary, "you woke up Baby Jasper. I just got him to sleep."

Kathy had an uneasy feeling that while Mrs. Young was talking to the dog, she was really looking at Kathy out of the corner of her eye. Rosemary was barking too loud to hear the "bad dog." Baby Jasper was crying almost as loud as Rosemary was barking.

Romeo stood up in Kathy's basket; his back was arched. Rosemary pushed her nose through the door

just as Romeo leapt from the basket and ran out the gate. Rosemary lunged through the door and ran after him.

"Oh, dear," Mrs. Young said, "who left the gate open? I'll have to get Rosemary before she knocks over a garbage can. We've been warned twice by the police."

"Mommeeee!" Baby Jasper cried.

The telephone began to ring. Mrs. Young looked around as if she'd never heard all these noises before.

"Did your mother want something, Kathy?" she asked as she ran out the door after Rosemary.

"No, no, I just . . ." Kathy said as she ran after Mrs. Young.

Romeo had climbed up the mulberry tree in Kathy's front yard.

Rosemary was standing on her hind legs with her front paws against the tree, barking at Romeo. Romeo stood on the first branch, just out of reach, and spit at Rosemary.

Mrs. Young grabbed hold of Rosemary's collar and started to pull her backward toward the Youngs' house. Rosemary kept straining until Mrs. Young had pulled her inside the fence and locked the gate.

Kathy could still hear the telephone ringing and Baby Jasper crying. She could tell from the traveling barks along the fence that Rosemary was running back and forth, angry at Romeo. Then the telephone stopped in the middle of a ring. Mrs. Young had answered it.

"I think I would have chosen to quiet Baby Jasper first," Kathy said to Romeo, who had climbed down from the tree. "He's much noisier than a telephone and won't stop on his own the way a telephone will."

Kathy took Romeo back to her house. "I hope I'm not too late for the Drum and Bugle Corps parade at Happy Hollow Park."

She slipped Romeo inside the door and called to her mother, "What time is it?"

"You've only been gone five minutes," her mother said.

Kathy thought this over. "I've decided against your staying with the Youngs," she said to Romeo. "If five minutes lasts that long at their house, imagine how long a year would last."

5

Just two days left! Romeo looked very worried. As soon as Kathy put her sandwich into her basket, he jumped in right on top of it. As she finished PBS14, Kathy decided to try the Olafs. They had no cats or dogs, and, sadly, no young children either. However there was always someone home. The Olafs worked shifts. When the little white sports car was parked in the driveway, Mr. Olaf was home and Mrs. Olaf was at work. When the big black station wagon was parked in the driveway, Mrs. Olaf was home and Mr. Olaf was at work. In between, at any hour of the day or night, their grown-up son would zoom in on his motorcycle. He was the youngest grown-up on the block. Maybe he still remembered about cats.

Romeo curled his two front paws under his chin and went to sleep as Kathy carried him to the Olafs' house. Kathy rang the bell. Mr. Olaf opened the door.

He filled the whole doorway up to the top and between both sides, almost like a giant. He blinked out at the sun, not seeing Kathy right away.

"Here I am," Kathy said.

"Ho, ho," Mr. Olaf laughed. "What are you doing way down there?"

Kathy thought of something funny that people always said to her dad.

"How's the weather up there?" she asked.

"Ho, ho, ho," Mr. Olaf laughed. "That's a good one."

Mr. Olaf shouted so loud that Romeo put his head up over the basket.

"Is that your cat?"

Kathy patted Romeo. Romeo stretched his neck out.

"Yes," Kathy said. She was proud of the white ruff of fur on his neck.

"Would he like to come here to live?" Mr. Olaf asked.

"Why, um . . ." Kathy was surprised Mr. Olaf had guessed why she had come.

Mr. Olaf flung his arm and pointed to the inside of his house.

"We need a cat for all these mice," he said.

Kathy looked in. The shades were drawn in the living room. She thought she saw one mouse behind the table leg but she was not sure. Romeo began to strain against her hand.

"A good mouser, that's what I need," Mr. Olaf

shouted. "Do you have mice at your house?"

"No," Kathy said sadly. She rather liked mice.

Mr. Olaf hit his fist in the palm of his hand. His round blue eyes were on Romeo.

"You know why you don't have mice? Because you have a cat! That's what I tell Dora, my wife. We need a cat to get rid of these pesky mice. These mice wouldn't be jumping on our dinner table and crawling over us at night if we had a good mouser."

Mr. Olaf paused and pointed at Romeo, who was getting quite restless in the basket.

"All day and all night they pester us," Mr. Olaf continued. "We're a two-shift family here. Each day is like two days. Even the mice have day and night shifts. Your cat would never go hungry here."

Kathy felt a little sick.

"Romeo eats Kitty Peppo Nuggets and drinks a bowl of warm milk at bedtime," she said.

"Not here, he wouldn't," Mr. Olaf shouted. "You can't pamper a cat or you ruin him as a mouser. He wouldn't get a bite here except what he could catch for himself. A real life for a real cat. That's what he'd have here."

Romeo pushed against Kathy's hand, leapt out of the basket, and ran home, straight up to the top of the mulberry tree.

30

"Look at him go!" Mr. Olaf said admiringly. "He's faster than any mouse we've got. How much do you want for him, little girl? I'd be willing to pay a fair amount. We're a working family here. I understand what a fair wage is."

It was just as if someone had asked Kathy's mother how much she wanted for Kathy—and meant it!

Kathy turned to run after Romeo. She felt like climbing a tree herself. "I think I'll be going. Good-bye," she called over her shoulder.

"Come over anytime," Mr. Olaf called loudly. "Bring your cat. There will always be someone here— day or night. We're a two-shift family. It makes each day seem twice as long."

Kathy sat down on the curb in front of her house while she waited for Romeo to come down from the tree.

"Romeo," she said to him when he was back on her lap, "you could never stay at the Olafs' house. Each day is like two days. I will find you a house where the days go fast."

But in spite of what Kathy said, she did not *know* that she could find a house for Romeo where the time went fast. And tomorrow night they were catching a plane for London.

6

At noon on June first, Romeo jumped into the basket on top of the sandwich, but Kathy didn't even stop at the curb to eat it. She walked straight down the block past the Youngs' and past the Olafs' to Mrs. Welk's house, the last one on the block, the only house left without a cat.

But she had little hope for Mrs. Welk, who lived all by herself. Sometimes Kathy saw her sitting on the porch swing with her toes barely touching the floor and her eyes closed. Sometimes after school Kathy would see her hand dart out to get the newspaper just as the newsboy came up to the porch.

"I bet each day lasts a hundred years here," Kathy said to Romeo. "But this is as far as I can go."

No cars were parked in the driveway. No toys were lying on the walk in front for Kathy to step over, and no dog barked at the window. Kathy and Romeo went under an arch with rose vines growing over it. The vines were covered with buds.

Mrs. Welk answered the door. She was a little round woman with a wrinkled face and curly white hair. She threw up her hands in surprise.

"My! My!" she said. "Come in and sit down. You must be tired, carrying your cat in that basket. Did you come a long way?"

Kathy laughed at the idea of Romeo's being a heavy load. "I am Kathy Spry," she said. "I live on the other side of the Youngs."

"Kathy Spry! Imagine that! It seems like just last summer you were napping in your buggy on the porch," Mrs. Welk said.

Kathy laughed again. Mrs. Welk made up funnier jokes than her father.

"I am going into the fourth grade next September, Mrs. Welk."

Everything seemed to surprise Mrs. Welk. "Imagine that," she said. "Going into the fourth grade already, and you walked all the way here on your lunch hour. You must be *very* tired. First, come into the kitchen. I think I have a sardine in the refrigerator for your cat. Then you and I will have a cup of tea. I have just made it. After tea I must take a half-hour nap before I make lunch. This is indeed a busy day!"

"Is your mother here?" Kathy asked.

She couldn't imagine anyone taking a nap in the

middle of the day unless his or her mother insisted.

"No, no. My mother has been gone many a year now," she said.

"I'm sorry," Kathy said. "But then why do you take a nap?"

"My daughter, who is a doctor, says that at my age I should take a nap every day, and so I do. In some ways my daughter seems to know best," Mrs. Welk said.

Kathy pictured herself wearing a stethoscope and saying to her mother, "You go right upstairs and take a nap."

She didn't think her mother would obey.

Kathy followed Mrs. Welk into her tiny kitchen. She could hear the clock tick. I couldn't live with all this quiet, she thought. Each day would last a thousand years.

Mrs. Welk took the sardine out of the refrigerator. Romeo grabbed it from her hand. The sound of his chomps filled the room, and then he swallowed the sardine with a noisy gulp.

Mrs. Welk looked at Romeo. "If I had a cat like that," she said, "he would save me the trouble of putting my leftover sardines into plastic bags and storing them in the refrigerator."

Kathy knew that Romeo could never stand the quiet

in Mrs. Welk's house. The quiet made Kathy's and Romeo's every move seem noisy. When they went into the living room, Romeo curled up by the fireplace and breathed noisily, almost snoring. Kathy's rocking chair creaked. Kathy sipped her tea with the smallest sips in the world, but they still sounded like slurps. She was glad she didn't have to chew any celery.

Mrs. Welk didn't seem to notice the noises that Kathy and Romeo were making. She smiled at Romeo.

"A cat dresses up a living room," she said. "And one good thing about a cat is that you never have to dust it and polish it. A cat carries its own weight, keeps itself cleaned and shined."

Kathy was glad that Mrs. Welk liked Romeo, but, she thought, each day would last a million years in this house.

"What do you do here all day?" Kathy asked.

"What do I do?" Mrs. Welk repeated. "What do I do? I'm glad you asked me that question. I'm busy from morning till night with comings and goings."

Mrs. Welk looked very determined. "I cannot take on one more duty," she said fiercely. "The gas man comes once a month to read the meter. Every day at four o'clock I have to go out to the porch to get the newspaper. Then on Saturday morning the newsboy stops by to collect for the *entire* week. On top of that, believe it or not, my neighbor wants to give me an African violet plant to take care of."

That didn't really seem like so much to do, but Kathy nodded politely.

"Then there are the telephone calls," Mrs. Welk continued. "Every single night my daughter, the doctor, calls. 'Why don't you take two aspirins so you can sleep, Mom?' she says. 'Call me in the morning and let me know how you are.' "

Mrs. Welk almost snorted—at least it seemed so to Kathy—but she may have just sniffed. Noises sounded so much louder in this house.

" 'You think I have time for that?' I ask my daughter," Mrs. Welk went on. "I have to let her know that I cannot take on one more thing. She just doesn't understand all I have to do. She has an office nurse who is paid good money to dial the office telephone and to pour out glasses of water for aspirins."

Mrs. Welk stopped talking then and smiled. The wrinkles on her face curved upward at both ends.

"Well," Mrs. Welk said, "it keeps me from getting old."

Mrs. Welk looked very old to Kathy, but she didn't say anything.

"Look outside in front," Mrs. Welk said. "See those rose vines growing over the trellis? As if there weren't

enough going on in this house, in two weeks all those roses will bloom at once."

Mrs. Welk yawned. "I get tired thinking about it," she said.

Kathy felt peaceful sitting in the chair. But she was sad that she hadn't found a home for Romeo. Mrs. Welk's house was out of the question. Not only did time creep by in her house, but Mrs. Welk wouldn't take on one more thing.

I still have the rest of my lunch hour, Kathy thought. I wish I knew someone else to try.

She got up to get Romeo, who was still sleeping soundly in front of the fireplace. At the same time she looked at the clock on the mantel. It was three minutes to one!

"I'm late, Mrs. Welk. I have to go!"

"Leave your cat here," Mrs. Welk said. "I'll put him out when I get the paper. A person learns to save energy in this house!"

"I'll come and get him," Kathy called as she ran out the door. She wanted to take no chance of Romeo's wandering away before they left.

Her mother was standing on the porch looking down the block, and Kathy waved to her as she ran by. She ran all the way to school and slipped into her seat just as the bell rang. Her stomach grumbled a little bit, and she remembered that she hadn't eaten her peanut butter sandwich. Even though she was hungry, she was glad for two things. One, she had made it to school on time, and two, her stomach hadn't growled at Mrs. Welk's house. It would have sounded as if a herd of buffalo were coming right through the living room.

7

When Miss Drobish threw open the classroom windows and the whole class stood up to sing a summertime song, Kathy felt a little puff of winter air seep into her chest. She hadn't solved Romeo's problem.

At the end of school, she put her pencils and artwork into her basket on top of her peanut butter sandwich and left, barely saying good-bye to her friends. They all thought she was so lucky to be going to London that very night on a big airplane. All she wanted to do was stay home and take care of Romeo.

Kathy stopped in front of her driveway. She didn't want to go inside. Her dad had trimmed the evergreens and put her bicycle in the basement. The house looked as if it belonged to strangers already.

She kicked a stone past the Youngs' house. She wondered again if she should leave Romeo with the Youngs, even though five minutes had seemed like a whole hour when she was there. But it wouldn't work; Rosemary

Young never had been nice to Romeo and she never would be. Kathy wondered what made some dogs act like that.

Romeo would have to live with three strange girls and three strange cats. I hope they all have kind hearts, Kathy thought. She waved to her mother, who was hurrying past the window with some trash, and sat down on the curb. As soon as she saw Mrs. Welk's newsboy, she would pick up Romeo and bring him home.

Mr. Olaf backed out of his driveway. He honked his horn as he passed Kathy. "Remember my offer for your cat," he yelled out the car window.

"I remember it," Kathy said.

Would Romeo like the Olafs' house? She thought about the question for one minute. The answer came loud inside her head. *No!* Not only was each day like two at the Olafs', but Romeo would be starved in those double days. He would have to kill mice and *eat* them to stay alive!

Living with three strange girls and three strange cats, even if there were only one kind heart among them, would be better than eating mice to stay alive.

A few minutes later a dusty station wagon with California license plates passed Kathy very slowly. The car stopped, backed up, and parked right in front

of Kathy's house. A grumpy-looking, long-haired white cat with blue eyes looked out the tailgate window. Holding the cat was a girl about eleven years old, with freckles, fat cheeks, and an angry face. She sat in the rear of the station wagon with her back to the rest of her family.

Another funny-looking cat had his face up to the side window. He was held by a girl about Kathy's age. He was a thin, pale cat with a dark face and a coat of fur that was darker at the edges, as if he were a tan cat turning black or a black cat turning tan. The girl who held him had one fist up to her eyes and she was crying.

Near the window on the other side was a little girl about five years old with light hair and a thin face. She held the oddest cat Kathy had ever seen. All the cats in the family were funny-looking, but this poor cat had no tail! Kathy tried not to stare.

The mother looked like all mothers, except that she was sneezing. She had red eyes and kept dabbing a wet handkerchief at them.

The father was rather hairy, and he was short for a father. He threw open the door of the car and all sorts of wails seemed to escape from inside.

This was going to be Romeo's family for a year. So far, Kathy rather liked them, in spite of the crying, sneezing, and grumpiness going on inside the car. Her family sometimes cried, sneezed, and got grumpy, too, especially on long car trips.

If, she said to herself, they'll give homes to such funny-looking cats, they must have very kind hearts, and they'll think Romeo is beautiful with his yellow striped coat and his bushy tail.

But the father, who bounded out of the car as if he were sitting on a hot stove, scared Kathy with his first words.

"If anyone so much as mentions the word *cat* to me, I'll sell all three of these cats to the highest bidder tomorrow morning."

The girls all wailed at once. Kathy wanted to comfort the girls and tell them that no one would pay money for such funny-looking cats.

Maybe the mother likes cats, Kathy thought.

The sneezing mother and the father who didn't want to hear the word *cat* again started to the house.

The father called to Kathy, "We want to pick up the keys. Are your folks around?"

"They're inside," she said.

The three girls got out of the car and Kathy went to meet them.

"I'm Angela," the big, angry girl said. She pointed to her long-haired white cat. "This is Ali Baba. He's a real Persian cat."

Kathy was surprised to hear that there *was* a real cat of any kind under all that hair. But she was polite. She reached out and petted Ali Baba.

"He has nice fur," she said.

The girl Kathy's age was still crying. "I am Susie," she sobbed. "This is Thai."

She held the cat in one hand and traced the dark edges of the cat's fur with her other hand. "He is a Siamese cat and cost *one hundred dollars*. He is the best cat in the family. So there!"

She stamped her foot at her big sister, Angela.

"You just keep quiet," Angela said, "or I'll tell Mom."

The littlest girl, who was holding the cat with no tail, showed her cat to Kathy. "I'm Tracy. My cat has no tail. My cat is the best cat in the whole world because she has no tail."

"Oh," Kathy said.

"I call her Maxine," the little girl said. "She's a Manx cat. See?"

She kept pointing at Maxine's back where her tail should have been.

If Tracy had been older, Kathy would have told her she shouldn't talk about people's or cats' shortcomings that way.

"What kind of a cat do you have?" the big girl asked Kathy.

"My cat is a yellow striped tabby cat," Kathy said, trying not to sound boastful. "He is ten years old."

"Oh," the big girl said, her nose going up a little bit in the air, "an alley cat. Some alley cats are very nice, I've heard."

"If I didn't have a 100 percent pure Siamese cat," the girl Kathy's age said, "I think I could like an alley cat."

"It's just a plain old cat," the littlest girl said. She hadn't learned to be polite yet. "With a plain old tail," she added.

Kathy could tell that even the polite girls didn't think much of a tabby cat. All three girls gathered together as if it were the first time they had agreed on something since they left California.

Kathy was glad to see the grown-ups come out of the house.

"I collect cats to show," the girls' father was saying to Kathy's dad. "But these kids are driving me crazy. They fight all the time about who has the best cat. Each girl will feed her own cat and nobody else's."

Kathy's eyes went to her dad's. He looked away.

"We keep the cats inside so they don't get into any

fights and tear their coats. I wouldn't put up with a cat who fought," the girls' father continued.

Kathy walked over to the sneezing mother. "Do you like cats?" she asked her.

She patted Kathy's head with one hand as she put a handkerchief to her nose with the other.

"I love cats!" she said between sneezes. "But I can have nothing to do with them. I'm allergic to all cats. Each of my girls has to keep her own cat in her own room. Being closed in the car with three cats all the way from California has really brought out my allergies."

She wiped her eyes, which were swollen and red. "I think your father said your cat likes to stay outside. I'll see that he's fed," she said kindly.

Kathy looked over at her dad. It was true that Romeo liked to stay outside, but he wasn't *kept* out. Her dad stooped down to tie his shoelace.

"We'll be back tonight after you leave," the girls' father said as they drove off.

Kathy saw the newsboy at the end of the block. She ran down the street to pick up Romeo, her basket jiggling at her side. She could hardly see as she ran. Her eyes were as filled with tears as the sneezing mother's had been. Romeo was going to spend the longest year of his life living with girls who called him an alley cat, a mother who wanted him to stay outside all the time, and a father who would not put up with him if he scratched another cat or tore its fur.

"Kathy! Wait!" her father called after her. "We're leaving in an hour."

But Kathy kept running, pretending she didn't hear him. Her mother and father had failed her. And she had failed Romeo.

8

When Mrs. Welk opened the door and Romeo stepped out, Kathy was there to pick him up. Romeo was licking his mouth. Mrs. Welk smiled.

"You're here already? I vow I don't know where the time goes. Come in for a few minutes to rest before you start your walk home," Mrs. Welk said. "I have the tea ready."

Something clicked in Kathy's head as she carried Romeo into Mrs. Welk's front hallway. But suddenly she was so hungry she could not think. As soon as she sat down at the little kitchen table, she took out her peanut butter sandwich and offered half of it to Mrs. Welk.

"Oh, thank you," Mrs. Welk said. Her tiny hand closed over it. As they both munched Kathy began to think again.

"You mean the three hours went fast?"

"Minutes, hours, days, all the same. They fly by. I don't know where they go," Mrs. Welk said. "This is

a very good peanut butter sandwich," she added.

Kathy was doubtful, not about the peanut butter sandwich, but about the minutes, hours, and days going fast.

"How about weeks, months, and years?"

"Exactly the same. I've no more packed away my Christmas tree lights when Groundhog Day is here; then it's General Grant's birthday; then summer comes and the days fly by, and lo and behold, it's the Feast of the Hunter's Moon and time to start addressing my Christmas cards. Then the year starts all over again."

There was another click in Kathy's head. It was a louder click than before because she was sitting right inside Mrs. Welk's house where all noises were so much louder. With this click an important thought flickered in Kathy's head.

Mrs. Welk took another bite of her half of the peanut butter sandwich.

"It must be forty years since I've had a peanut butter sandwich," Mrs. Welk said. "Seems like yesterday."

Kathy was thinking that if the time went so fast for Mrs. Welk, maybe it would go fast for Romeo, too. But no, she remembered, Mrs. Welk was too busy to take on one more duty.

"A person gets too busy to make peanut butter sand-wiches," Mrs. Welk said. "I just have too many things to do. I keep telling my daughter I cannot add one more duty to my day."

Kathy's last hope was gone. With a loud clatter, she pushed her chair away from the table and picked Romeo up off the floor.

"Well, good-bye," she said. "Thank you for taking care of Romeo when you are so busy."

"Busy!" Mrs. Welk mumbled, her mouth full. "You don't know the half of it!"

Kathy was about to start crying again. She stood fumbling with her basket, not wanting to pick it up, not wanting to go home. She wanted to run away someplace with Romeo and never come back. She couldn't swallow the last bite of her peanut butter sandwich because her throat didn't seem to work right.

But all of a sudden, Mrs. Welk looked different. She had stopped talking as she ate her last few bites of PBS15. She got up slowly from the table and her face turned very sad. The wrinkles were still there, but for a moment it seemed to Kathy that Mrs. Welk's eyes looked like her own.

"Mrs. Welk," Kathy said, "I have to say good-bye. My mother and father and I are going to London for the year."

"But who," asked Mrs. Welk, almost fiercely, "will look after Romeo?"

Kathy finally swallowed her last bit of the sandwich—and then she realized something. Mrs. Welk hadn't asked about airplanes or Big Ben or castles. *Mrs. Welk was a grown-up who remembered about cats.*

"Mrs. Welk, would . . ." But Kathy's voice trailed off as she thought about how busy Mrs. Welk was.

Then Kathy thought of something her dad always said: "If you want something done, ask a busy person." She took a deep breath.

"Mrs. Welk, would you look after Romeo?"

Mrs. Welk seemed shocked. She sat down on a kitchen chair and looked at Kathy. A little light that hadn't been there before flickered in her eyes.

The air was very quiet, even for Mrs. Welk's house. All three of them, including Romeo, were holding their breath.

"Cats are like peanut butter sandwiches," Mrs. Welk said at last. "One gets so busy, one forgets how nice they are. It's a strange thing, Kathy, but I realized this afternoon that Romeo is livelier and less trouble than an African violet. He doesn't need to have special lamps or to be watered. In any contest, Romeo would win over an African violet, hands down."

Kathy, Mrs. Welk, and Romeo all smiled at once. Mrs. Welk stood up. She stopped smiling and looked very determined.

"Yes. Yes. I will. I will look after Romeo. He will help me with my work," and then Mrs. Welk continued so softly that Kathy could hardly hear her, "and keep me company."

Click, click, click, clunk! Everything fell into place with a loud *clunk* inside Kathy's head. She was sure it echoed through the whole house. But she didn't care. She reached out and hugged Mrs. Welk with one arm, squashing Romeo between them.

"You want to look after Romeo, Mrs. Welk? You honestly do? You aren't too busy?" she asked. "Romeo wouldn't be another duty? Really? And the time does go fast here? Truly?"

The surprised Mrs. Welk and Kathy and Romeo all hugged one another at once. (Actually Romeo just managed to hang on.) The happy noises echoed from the front door to the back door and in and out of all the rooms in between.

Mrs. Welk and Kathy had solved Romeo's problem on the fifteenth peanut butter sandwich. But Romeo had done his part, too. It turned out he had helped Mrs. Welk all afternoon while Kathy was in school. He had finished her tuna fish at lunchtime so she didn't have to put it away in the refrigerator. He had licked up the drops of cream she had spilled on the kitchen floor when she made her tea. Best of all, he had jumped in and out of her lap without her having to stoop to pick him up and put him down.

"He's a cat who carries his own weight and more," Mrs. Welk said.

Before Kathy's father would agree to dropping Romeo off at Mrs. Welk's for a whole year, he called Dr. Welk.

"Dr. Welk is happy to have her mother keep Romeo," Mr. Spry said as he hung up. "She worries all the time about Mrs. Welk's not having anything to do all day."

Dr. Welk doesn't even know about the gas man, the newsboy, and the roses blooming all at once, Kathy thought. Daughters don't always know everything, especially when they grow up. Kathy smiled down at Romeo, who was curled up asleep on her lap. He seemed to be smiling in his sleep.

Kathy's dad picked up the bag of Kitty Peppo Nuggets and Romeo's bed.

"Good job, Kathy," he said. "Jolly good job. Jolly, jolly good."

Jolly good indeed, Kathy thought.

She carried Romeo into the kitchen and placed a half-finished jar of peanut butter in a bag. Then they all started down to Mrs. Welk's. With the help that

Romeo was going to give her, Mrs. Welk would have time to make a peanut butter sandwich now and then.

Kathy told her that it would be all right if she sat on the porch swing to solve Romeo's problems, instead of on the curb.

"And don't give up, Mrs. Welk. Never give up." Kathy reached over and took Mrs. Welk's freckled hand. "Even if it takes *sixteen peanut butter sandwiches!*"